SHADE

RISING TIDE

The boy looked down at his own feet. Water oozed between his toes. He didn't move any part of his body except his eyes. Chris felt ashamed. He shouldn't have said that. Lots of people couldn't afford stuff. His family only had just enough and that was because of the money his dad earned in the army.

'Are you a climref?' he asked. And the boy ran.

Look out for other exciting stories
in the *Shades* series:

A Murder of Crows by Penny Bates
Animal Lab by Malcolm Rose
Blitz by David Orme
Coming In To Land by Dennis Hamley
Cry, Baby by Jill Atkins
Cuts Deep by Catherine Johnson
Danger Money by Mary Chapman
Doing the Double by Alan Durant
Fighting Back by Helen Bird
Fire! by David Orme
Four Degrees More by Malcolm Rose
Gateway from Hell by John Banks
Hauntings by Mary Chapman
Hunter's Moon by John Townsend
Life of the Party by Gillian Philip
Mantrap by Tish Farrell
Mind's Eye by Gillian Philip
Nightmare Park by Philip Preece
Plague by David Orme
The Scream by Penny Bates
Shouting at the Stars by David Belbin
Space Explorers by David Johnson
Tears of a Friend by Joanna Kenrick
The Messenger by John Townsend
Treachery by Night by Ann Ruffell
Virus by Mary Chapman
Who Cares? by Helen Bird
Witness by Anne Cassidy

SHADES

RISING TIDE

Anne Rooney

With thanks to Luke O'Keefe, for the gravy.

Published by Evans Brothers Limited
2A Portman Mansions
Chiltern St
London W1U 6NR

First published in 2009

British Library Cataloguing in Publication Data
Rooney, Anne.
Rising tide. -- (Shades)
1. Young adult fiction.
I. Title II. Series
823.9'2-dc22

ISBN-13: 9780237539481

Editor: Julia Moffatt
Designer: Rob Walster

Chapter One

The water was dark and choppy far beneath him. Danny swung himself on to the safety rail running along the deck. Should he dive or jump? The tanker cut easily through the surf. Far off on his left, a few lights gleamed, marking the south English coast. Ahead, he could make out the first of the patrol boats, darker shapes in the darkness. Danny's bare feet curled around the cold metal rail. It was slippery with sea water. He gripped the top rail with his hands, then twisted round to face the water. He had to get as far from the boat as possible so that he wouldn't be pulled under. He took a deep breath, and threw himself into the sea, far below.

The cold water hit him like a hard slap, snatching his breath away. It was nothing like the warm ocean at home where he had practised for months for this moment. This stung his whole body. Gritting his teeth, he sliced through the water, moving up and down with the swell. It would take a couple of hours to reach those lights on the shore. And then he'd have to veer to the left. He had to come ashore where there were no lights, no people. He'd studied maps online. The printed maps were no good now – the coastline changed so quickly. Since 2015, when everything had started to go wrong, few coastlines had stayed the same. Even here, in England, bits of it were being eaten away by the rising sea. Who knew how long this land would last?

Danny knew where he was heading. He'd picked a place with a shallow beach. He'd checked the satellite pictures from the bridge of the tanker that morning so he knew it was still there. He could walk up the beach and hide until daybreak. Maybe his clothes would dry, too, if it was hot. Then he'd make his way into town. And then? He didn't know. Find somewhere to sleep, first, and get some food from someone. He could plan while he was swimming. He had plenty of time.

Behind him the water tanker disappeared into the darkness. No one had raised the alarm – no shout of 'man overboard', no gun shots. Head down and swim. He was on his way.

Chapter Two

It was the first time the water had come through the ground. It bubbled up where Chris's feet pressed into the turf. Swilling and swirling, it first filled the dents made by his studs and then his whole footprint. His football boots made a squelching sound as he ran, the wet ground sucking on his feet.

Almost the same time as he noticed the water, he saw the African. Tall and dark and slim, the African stood in the trees like a shadow. Chris thought him beautiful, in a way. There was something quiet and poised about him. He didn't move, but just looked out at the boys playing football on the wet grass.

It hadn't rained for weeks. The sun had been hotter than ever, the hottest yet of these hot summers. The water came from nowhere. Chris wondered if a pipe had burst. That must be it. What a waste, when they had to be so careful with water now.

'We can't play like this, lads,' Coach Engers called out. 'Change out of your strip and go home. I'll see you all on Friday.'

Some of the kids grumbled. They needed to practise for Saturday's match. If they didn't win, they'd be out of the league. Chris didn't care about the practice, but he didn't want to go home. He knew what it would be like. His sister Katie shut in her room, or complaining about everything. His little brother, Edgar, watching re-runs of old Cartoon Network series. His mother. If she was in, she'd be drinking cider in the kitchen and doing sudoku puzzles. And getting them wrong. If there was to be dinner, he'd have to make it.

So while the other boys kicked the ball towards the changing area, Chris walked between the trees. The African didn't move, but looked straight at Chris. His eyes shone. He looked like a gazelle in a wildlife documentary the moment before it runs from the lion – frozen, alert. Chris held out his hand.

'Wait,' he said. 'Don't go.'

Still the boy didn't move or speak.

'You're not from round here, are you?' Chris asked. 'I've never seen you before. Do you speak English?'

Still he didn't speak.

Chris could see him more clearly now. The boy was his age, maybe a year or two older – seventeen at most. He was very thin. He wore a torn, dark blue t-shirt, dirty sweat pants that were too short, no shoes.

'You're not wearing any shoes,' Chris said.

The boy looked down at his own feet. Water oozed between his toes. He didn't move any part of his body except his eyes. Chris felt ashamed. He shouldn't have said that. Lots of people couldn't afford stuff. His family only had just enough and that was because of the money his dad earned in the army.

'Are you a climref?' he asked. And the boy ran.

Chapter Three

'Wait!' Chris called into the emptiness between the trees. 'I won't tell!' But there was only silence, and the squelching of his own football boots as he took a few steps after the running boy. No good – he was gone.

By the time Chris got home, Edgar was already eating in front of the TV.

Cornflakes and gravy. Yum. Their mother was out. That was a relief, but she'd be a pain when she got back later – if she came back at all tonight. Chris cooked pasta, stirred tomato paste through it and took his bowl to sit with Edgar.

'OK, Peanut?' he asked Edgar. Edgar nodded and smiled at him, then took a bit of pasta from Chris's bowl.

'You finished with that?' Chris asked, pointing at the soggy cornflakes. Edgar nodded again.

Chris carried the bowls out to the dustbin. He couldn't leave them in the kitchen or the rats would come in. It was already dusk. The air was like a blanket, hot and thick. As he walked to the bin, Chris saw a shadow under the lamppost. Not that the lamps were ever on any more. They hadn't been turned on for five years now. The shadow was tall and slim, poised to run away. The boy from the park.

'Don't go,' Chris said again. He would have held out his hands, but he had the bowls. The African looked at him, then looked at the bowls. Chris's bowl was empty. Edgar's bowl held a brownish sludge of soggy cornflakes and gravy. The boy licked his lips.

'No,' said Chris. 'It's rubbish. You wouldn't like it.'

He went quickly to the bin and scraped Edgar's bowl. In a flash, the boy was beside him, reaching into the bin.

'NO!' shouted Chris. The boy jumped back, startled. Chris saw that he was thinner than just thin. 'Wait. I'll get you something if you're hungry.'

The boy smiled, but still said nothing.

'Wait there,' Chris said again. He

returned a moment later with four slices of white bread smeared with margarine. The boy crammed them into his mouth, slice after slice. They were gone in seconds.

'More?' Chris asked. The boy smiled. So Chris brought him more, and stood waiting as he ate it.

'That happened in my country, the water,' the boy said. Chris jumped. He'd got used to his silence.

'The water came up through the ground. First when we ran, then all the time. Then everywhere. Our houses fell down. Our streets washed away. Nothing would grow. No food. We had to leave.'

'Your country?' asked Chris. 'You're not from England, then?'

'No.' The boy licked the last smears of margarine from his fingers. He looked eagerly at Chris.

'You can't have more now,' Chris said. 'If you haven't eaten, you need to start slowly. Your stomach can't take too much at once. Come back in the morning, before school.'

Before Chris had finished speaking, the boy had slipped into the darkness.

Chapter Four

Next morning, the boy was there when Chris pulled the curtains back. It startled Chris. The hedge hid him from the road. Even though it was dying and brown, it was still thick. Chris wondered how long he'd been there, waiting, behind the curtains. It made him uneasy. He didn't like to think of the boy standing unseen the other side of the glass. He went to the kitchen to get more bread, then thought again and took cornflakes and milk. The boy took it and emptied the bowl in seconds. He wiped his finger around it and licked the milk from his finger.

'Thank you,' he said. Chris thought that was a good sign.

'What's your name?' he asked. 'I'm Chris.'

The boy smiled.

'Danny.'

Edgar came up behind Chris.

'Who's that? Where are my cornflakes?' he said. 'Is that your friend?'

Chris looked at Danny.

'Yes,' he said, 'he's my friend. He's called Danny.'

'Then why doesn't he come in?' Edgar asked. Chris looked at Danny, then waved him in.

Danny stood looking around him. He looked down at the carpet under his feet and wriggled his toes.

'You don't have any shoes,' said Edgar.

'No,' said Danny. 'I don't have anything much.'

Katie appeared in the doorway, a slice of toast in her hand.

'He's a climref, isn't he?' she said. 'Of course he doesn't have shoes. What's he doing here?'

'He's my friend,' Chris said quickly. 'And he's not a climref.'

Katie shrugged.

'Whatever.'

'Are you a climref?' asked Edgar.

Danny looked at Chris.

'What's a climref?' he asked.

'Climate refugee. Someone who's run away from their country because of problems caused by climate change,' explained Chris.

'Someone who shouldn't be here,' added Edgar. 'We don't have climrefs here, though. They're all in London and Southampton. Aren't they?'

Chris nodded, but said nothing. It wasn't true. They were everywhere. Even in the living room, now.

'Come on, Peanut, time for school,' Chris said. 'See you later, Danny.' He opened the door for Danny to leave, taking the cereal bowl from his hand. When he turned, Katie was leaning in the doorway to the kitchen.

'Are you going to turn him in?' she asked.

'No,' Chris said quickly. 'Of course not. He's not a climref. He's just – new here.'

'He hasn't got any shoes. You gave him food. Since when?'

'Lots of people can't afford shoes. Don't

jump to conclusions.'

He was worried, though.

'He's a climref, stupid,' she said, and carried on staring at him. Chris picked up his bag.

'Don't report him,' Chris said. 'Please.'

But Katie just shrugged and watched as Chris picked up his bag and followed Edgar out of the door.

Chapter Five

After school, Chris went through the park. Several of the team were there, though they hadn't arranged to train. They didn't have their strip or boots, but someone had brought a ball. They marked out goals with their bags and began kicking around, practising moves, passing, dribbling. Soon,

Chris saw Danny between the trees.

'Come and play,' Chris called to him. 'Do you know how to play football?'

Danny nodded.

'Is it OK?'

'Sure – we're only messing around. The ground's soft, though.'

Danny stepped out on to the grass and all the boys looked at him. They looked at his feet, damp and bare, pressing into the grass and making the water pool around them.

'Guys, this is Danny. He's – he's from – Chiswick.'

A couple of the boys raised a hand in dumb greeting.

'Chiswick, d'you say? Do you play in the team, then?'

It was Pierce. Pierce was a poor player, and a bully. Chris didn't like him – none of the team liked him. But they had no reserve. If they didn't have him, they didn't play the league.

'Do you?' Pierce tried again. Danny looked at Chris. It was a confused, pleading look.

'No,' said Chris quickly. 'He hasn't any boots. He can't join the team.'

Pierce curled his lip and sneered at Danny's feet.

'Let's play,' Chris said quickly, before Pierce could start anything.

For a few minutes, Danny hung around the sidelines, running in now and again, then retreating. He didn't go near the ball. Chris wondered if he really did know how to play. But then, suddenly, he was in. Running and darting and lunging, making graceful long kicks that sent the ball soaring. It took Chris's breath away. A couple of the lads stopped and watched him.

After twenty minutes, they stopped for a

breather. Some of them, Pierce included, puffed and sweated in the heat. Danny didn't even raise a sweat. He smiled at them as they rested. Pierce scowled at him.

'What you staring at? Anything strange?'

Danny shook his head.

'So. Danny.' Pierce gave a twisted smile, more a grimace. 'My uncle lives in Chiswick. You might know him. What street d'you live in?'

Danny's eyes flashed towards Chris, who came to his rescue.

'Come on guys, let's play more.' He kicked the ball to Pierce, who slipped on the wet grass and fell heavily. Pierce swore, got up, and ran furiously to tackle Danny, who now had the ball. Danny passed to Simon, a swift, elegant kick. And Pierce stamped hard on Danny's bare toes.

'Ooh, so sorry mate,' Pierce smirked.

Danny froze, his eyes filled with pain, and his mouth a thin line. Chris ran over. He looked down. The water that oozed up between Danny's toes was red with blood. Two of Danny's toenails were crushed into the pulpy flesh. Chris clenched his fists.

'I said sorry.' Pierce shrugged and smiled. There was nothing Chris could do. He couldn't fight Pierce – he stood no chance, and Pierce had mates who'd beat him up later.

'Why bother?' Pierce called as Chris helped Danny to a bench. 'He's only a climref, isn't he?'

Chapter Six

Chris helped Danny hobble home. He was anxious about it but there didn't seem to be much choice. He couldn't just send him off into the woods again, hungry and hurt and bleeding. But when they got there, Chris's mum was in. Drunk, as usual. Her tuneless singing leaked out of the door as soon as he opened it. Chris was too ashamed to take Danny in. He took him round to the back garden, into the shed.

'My mum's in,' he explained. 'She won't let you in. I'll bring you food. I'll get a sleeping bag too – just for tonight. OK?'

Danny nodded.

'Just like home,' he said.

Chris couldn't tell whether it was a joke or not.

The floor of the shed was wet. That wasn't right. The water must be coming up through the ground here, too.

Chris did what he could to fix Danny's toes. He used tweezers to remove the shattered bits of toenail where he could. Parts were still attached to the mash of toe beneath. Danny winced and sucked in his breath when Chris pulled even gently on those parts. He couldn't take him to a doctor – a doctor might turn him in. And it wouldn't just be Danny who was in trouble.

Chris decided not to mention Danny again. He hoped that Edgar and Katie – and especially Pierce – would forget about him.

But the next day, the first of the dead Africans turned up on the beach. The papers, the radio and TV, news websites – everything was covering the story. An illegal refugee ship had been sunk by patrol boats. It had no lifeboats. The authorities had rescued only a handful of climrefs from the sea. The rest were washing up with the tide, all along the coast. The beaches were immediately sealed. When Danny went to the park that evening, the boys were talking about it.

'Why did they fish them out at all?' asked Pierce. 'They should just have machine-gunned them – chh-chh-chh-chh-chh.'

He mimed a gunner, swinging round to pepper Chris with bullets. 'What are they doing over here?' he went on. 'There's no room in this country for everyone who wants to run away.'

No one liked to disagree with Pierce. It was hard to tell who thought he was right and who was just afraid to stand up to him.

'What do you think?' Pierce jabbed his finger hard into Chris's chest. It hurt. Chris stumbled backwards and Pierce took a step after him.

'Where's your climref, then?' He poked him again.

'He's not a climref,' Chris said, stepping back. 'And he's gone home.'

'To Chiswick?' sneered Pierce.

'Yes, to Chiswick.'

'Good riddance,' snarled Pierce.

They faced each other, Pierce flexing his

fingers, trying out a fist. Chris stood his ground but felt sick.

'Let's play!' called Simon, dropping the ball between them.

'Yeah, I was gonna play,' Pierce sneered. He lashed out with his foot and sent the ball soaring towards the trees, but he kept his eyes on Chris.

They kicked the ball around and water welled up under their feet. Chris hung back, well out of range.

'This sucks,' grumbled Pierce. 'We'll have to find somewhere else.'

'Uphill,' said Chris. 'It will have to be higher. The water comes from underground.'

'Yeah, we can see that, boff,' said Pierce, leaning toward him threateningly.

'Tomorrow, then,' Chris called over his shoulder as he turned away.

Chapter Seven

Just outside the park, Chris saw the police with riot shields. They were herding a troop of climrefs. Most were black, probably Africans, looking as poor as Danny. But about a third were white Europeans. They looked puzzled, as if they couldn't understand how this had happened. The police made Chris stand by the wall as they passed. One pointed his laser gun at Chris, making sure he stood well back. A woman carrying a small child was crying quietly. A man touched her elbow and asked the nearest police officer,

'Where are you taking us? We are EU citizens, we have free movement around Europe. We can go where we please.'

'Where are you from?' the police officer asked him.

'We are Dutch. From Amsterdam.'

'You'll go to Eurocamp 2, then – it's an EU camp. Now keep moving.'

'I am from Belgium,' said a black woman. 'I want to live in this country. It is allowed, no?'

'This country's full,' said the policeman. 'And the sea is rising here, too. Won't be long before people can't live here. You'll have to go to a camp. They're not so bad.'

He waved her along with his laser gun. Soon, the people had passed and Chris could make his way home. He went straight to the shed.

Danny was sitting on the floor. He'd found a garden knife and was making a wooden figure from a stick. It was pretty good, and Chris was impressed. Danny smiled at him.

'Not much to do in here,' he said.

'No, I'm sorry. I'll bring you some magazines, books,' Chris said. 'Let's clean up that foot. Can't afford to let it get infected.'

He took off the plasters he'd put on the day before. He talked to Danny while he cleaned the wounds, hoping to distract him from the pain.

'Why did you come here?'

Danny winced and clenched his fist.

'The ground was going. The water came up from underneath, like in your park. And when the tide was high, it flooded the land. But there was no rain, and the rivers were dry. There was lots of fighting. Everyone was trying to escape. The borders were closed. They shot at refugees who tried to cross.

I worked the water ships. We sailed north to fill tankers with water. It could never be enough, but it was something. We're never allowed to go on land when the tanker docks. Armed guards make sure no one jumps ship.'

'How did you get here, then?' Chris had finished cleaning away the dried blood and peered at the blackened remains of Danny's toe-nails. The light in the shed was poor. It was hard to tell how bad it was.

Danny looked away as Chris started to

put on fresh plasters. They were a plastic pink colour that looked ugly against Danny's velvety skin.

'I trained for months,' he continued. 'Swimming in the sea. Swimming and swimming until I could swim ten miles. The ships keep five miles from the shore. Any closer and they need an escort. So I jumped in the night and swam to shore. In these clothes.' He looked down at his ragged t-shirt.

'You swam five miles?' Chris was impressed, again. There was a lot that was impressive about Danny.

'Six. I didn't want to take a chance with the patrols, so I jumped early.'

Danny held his foot, now Chris had finished.

'Why did he do that?' Danny asked.

'Pierce? He's a bully.'

'But why?'

'You're better at football than he is. It annoyed him. And he doesn't think you should be here. You – all climrefs, from anywhere. He thinks you should be sent home.'

He didn't add that Pierce thought climrefs should be shot.

'But there is no home. No one can live there now.'

'Then he'd say you should die there.'

'I don't want to die. Anywhere. That's why I came here.'

'Why would you die?'

It was Edgar. He was standing in the doorway, eating cheap biscuits from the packet.

'My country is dying,' answered Danny. 'Everyone wants to leave, but there is nowhere to go. Rich people pay to go on boats.'

'They die, too,' said Edgar. 'Like that boat that sank. It was on the news. All the climrefs drowned. I saw a body—'

'Come on, Edgar,' interrupted Chris. 'Give Danny some biscuits and leave him in peace. Let's go indoors.'

Chapter Eight

Chris's mum was out again when the police came to the door. It was just as well. He said there was no one over eighteen in the house. The police would need to come back with a warrant.

'We have information that there's an illegal climate refugee at this address. Can you tell me whether that is the case?'

The policeman held his recorder out to catch Chris's answer. Chris knew his body language in the video shots would be analysed, too. He must give nothing away.

'I'm not aware of any climrefs here,' he said. 'But my mother's out. You'll have to come back later and ask her.'

The policeman swore under his breath. He couldn't go into the house if there were only minors there, but if there was a climref, he'd now given him the chance to get away.

'We'll be back tomorrow,' the officer said. 'The house will be under surveillance until then,' he added.

He attached a magnetic vidcam to the lamppost. He set it up to point at Chris's front door, then waved his hand in front of the lens to check it was picking up movement before he left.

Chris chewed his thumb thoughtfully. They could come back with a warrant. They'd find Danny sooner or later. Who had ratted on him? Katie? Pierce, most likely. Even though Pierce didn't know Danny was there, he'd enjoy causing trouble for Chris. And there would be trouble if the house were searched. They'd collect DNA and try to match it. Danny's DNA wouldn't be on the database.

'What about an ID?' Katie said, from behind him. Chris spun round.

'What?'

'A fake ID. Like the one you have to buy beer. Get Danny an ID and the police can't touch him.'

'How do you know I have a fake ID?'

Katie made a 'loser' sign at him and went back to her room. He hated to admit it, but it was a good idea. He could buy a photocard

ID for a couple of euros online. He could even get a DNA match ID for about twenty euros, but they'd have to wait for that – they'd have to send the sample and wait for the card. There wasn't time. But photo ID was a good start – it would get the police off Danny's back for a bit. He went out to the shed to take a photo of Danny to upload.

Chapter Nine

Pierce was standing by the shed.

'Chiswick the name of your shed is it?' he asked.

He was tossing half a brick from one hand to the other.

Chris swallowed.

'You got that climref in there, haven't you?'

Chris didn't answer.

'Oh, you got a camera? Nice. You can take the pictures while I beat his brains out. Then we can hand him over and collect the reward. Good plan, eh? And you can give me your share and I won't tell them you hid him. OK?'

Pierce dropped the brick next to his foot.

'Whoops. Could have hurt my toes then,' he said.

Chris clenched his free hand into a fist. Pierce glanced at the fist and twisted his mouth into a smile. He had a broken tooth, a reminder of a previous fight.

'Open up, then. Let's see how your climref's doing.'

Pierce kicked the door.

There was no choice. If Chris didn't open the door, Pierce would beat him up and then he'd still beat up Danny. He undid the catch on the shed door. As he did it, he felt cold water around his feet. Here, at the bottom of the garden, the water came halfway over his trainers.

'You stand there,' Pierce pointed to a place a few feet back from the door. 'And make sure you take a picture as soon as I open the door, to get his startled little face. Then put it on video while I beat the shit out of him.'

Chris felt sick. His head was swimming and his stomach churned. How could he stand there and film this? He nodded weakly. There was nothing else he could do. He should have turned Danny in. At least in a camp he would be safe.

Pierce held the broken brick high in one hand. He threw the shed door back with the other. For a moment, the gloom of the shed confused him. He couldn't make out Danny in the darkness. He couldn't make out the garden knife Danny held out in front of him – the garden knife that Chris's mother used to use to prune trees, long ago when she wasn't always wasted, and when there were proper seasons and trees grew. Pierce's hand with the brick came down hard towards Danny's head. Chris closed his eyes and without realising he pressed the button on the camera. The flash went off at the same moment as Danny dodged the brick and lunged with the knife.

The brick came down on the corner of a shelf, but Pierce had dropped it. His hand curled into a claw, and he let out a terrible shriek. Blood gushed from his leg, splashing on to the floor, on to Danny. Pierce crumpled forward. Danny still held the knife. He was shuddering, and his eyes flickered. Pierce's leg was caught in the lawn mower. The flash had blinded him and he hadn't seen the old mower. After a moment he crashed to the floor in front of Danny. He was bellowing in pain. The water that had seeped through the floor of the shed was red with blood. It swilled around Danny's bare feet.

'Come on out,' Chris said quietly. He held a hand out to Danny, to help him round Pierce's bulk. Danny was trembling. His sweatpants were spattered with blood.

'He would have half-killed you and then turned you in,' Chris said.

'Will he die?' Danny asked. His voice was cracking. He was almost in tears.

'Dunno,' said Chris. He took the knife from Danny and closed the shed door.

Chapter Ten

'What are we going to do?' Danny asked. 'We can't just leave him there. He might bleed to death.'

They sloshed their way along the path. The water was nearly up to their ankles and it was still rising.

Katie was in the kitchen with her

homework spread out on the table. There was a puddle of water by the back door. Katie didn't seem to have noticed it until Chris and Danny splashed through it. She glanced up, then pointed at the blood splattered over Danny.

'What happened to you?' she gasped.

'Not him – Pierce,' Chris cut in. 'He had a little accident in the shed. He's bleeding rather a lot.'

'And you left him there?' Katie was shocked. 'Call an ambulance, idiot!'

But she reached for her own phone. She punched in the number and asked for the ambulance service.

'What happened?' she asked. 'They want to know who, what, how, where.'

Chris took the phone from her.

'Hello there. There was a climref hiding in my shed. He was startled when I opened the door and he fell on a lawnmower. He's cut his leg. It looks bad, he's losing a lot of blood.'

'They'll be right over,' he said to Katie, handing her the phone. 'I'll go back out and check up on him till they come. Danny – stay out of the way for now.'

Chris sploshed his way back to the shed. He opened the door. Pierce was where he'd left him, looking very pale, drenched in blood. His leg was still trapped. He was leaning awkwardly against the wall. Chris reached inside Pierce's jacket and took out his wallet. He took the ID card and put the wallet back. Pierce made no effort to stop him. Chris stuffed the ID card in his pocket.

'Ambulance will be here soon,' he said to Pierce. 'They'll sort you out.'

At that moment, the ambulance crew arrived in the garden.

'This the climref?' asked the woman in front.

'Yeah – he was hiding in the shed. The police were looking for him. They came round earlier.'

'Excellent. Come on you, let's get you sorted out. That looks nasty. Do you speak English?'

Pierce was too weak to speak at all. He nodded.

'What will happen to him?' asked Chris.

The woman jabbed a needle into Pierce's leg. Pierce moaned.

'It'll stop hurting in a minute,' she said. Then she turned to Chris.

'We'll stitch him up, pump him full of antibiotics and send him off to Eurocamp 3.'

'Not climref,' Pierce managed to whisper.

'That's what they all say. We'll check your DNA in hospital. But even if you weren't before you are now – this whole area's been declared unlivable. Everyone's off to Ecocamp EU3. The evacuation squad are on their way.'

Chapter Eleven

Chris turned and ran, splashing water up behind him as he went. The woman looked after him, then shrugged and turned back to Pierce.

In the house, Chris grabbed things and stuffed them into a bag: a change of clothes for each of them, two packs of biscuits, a bottle of water, all their ID cards. Danny held the bag open for him. When he'd finished Chris took Pierce's ID card and pushed it into Danny's hand.

'Katie, Edgar, come NOW,' he shouted up the stairs.

To his surprise, they both came immediately.

'There's water in here,' said Edgar as he paddled into the kitchen.

'There's water everywhere,' said Chris. 'Now, you have to do as I say. We have to leave immediately. We have to get to the train station and take the train to Derby, to Uncle Al's farm. It's high up, it will be dry for a long time. It's not going to be easy. Everyone will be trying to leave.'

'What about Mum?' asked Edgar.

'I'll text her,' said Chris, 'tell her to meet us at the station. If we wait here, we'll all end up in the ecocamp.'

He led the other three out of the door and locked it.

They hurried to the street, splashing through the water. Chris glanced over his shoulder. At the bottom of the hill, the evacuation squad had just come round the corner. They were knocking on the first door. It would take a good half hour, dealing with complaints and the crying, before they got to Chris's house. The four of them should get to the station in time to get out, ahead of the rush. The water swirled around their ankles. Edgar stumbled, and Chris helped him up.

'I'll catch you up,' called Danny, and he ran back and round to the garden.

The woman from the ambulance was helping Pierce out of the shed. He still looked pale, but the painkillers had kicked in and he was complaining loudly that he wasn't a climref. A long line of stitches across his leg held the lips of the gash together.

'Wait,' called Danny. 'He's not a climref. Here's his ID. It's all a mistake. He must have dropped it.'

He held the ID card out to the woman. She looked at it, compared the photo with Pierce.

'I should run a DNA scan…' she started.

'No time,' said Danny, 'he can come with us. We'll look after him.'

Pierce opened his mouth to speak, but Danny shot him a warning look. He closed his mouth. The woman looked at him.

'You OK with that?'

Pierce nodded.

'Take these.' She handed him a bottle of pills. 'They're for the pain. And these –

they're antibiotics. Two a day. Now go before I change my mind.' She started to pack her things away. Danny darted past her.

'There's an old bike,' he said to Pierce, 'I saw it in the shed.' A moment later he'd dragged it out. With Pierce perched on the carrier behind him, Danny set off down the path after and up the road towards Chris, Edgar and Katie, climbing the hill to the station. Danny pedaled as fast as he could, but the tyres were flat and it was hard going.

'Wait!' he called. Chris turned. He put a hand on Edgar's shoulder to stop him. The three of them watched Danny and Pierce make slow progress up the hill. At last they caught up.

'Can't I go on the bike?' asked Edgar. 'It's too hard.'

'Sorry, Peanut,' said Chris. 'Pierce needs it more than you. It's not far to the station.'

'But Pierce did a bad thing.'

'We all do bad things now and then,' said Danny. 'He's learned a useful lesson. And we don't have to do bad things back.'

He shot a look at Pierce.

'Can you walk?' Chris asked Pierce. 'That bike's not much good.'

Pierce nodded, and they left the bike against a wall.

'Where will everyone else go?' Edgar asked.

'They'll go to ecocamps. Like the camps dad guards. They'll have to make things – wind turbines, solar panels – or build things – like power stations. It's not great. But it's not forever. They'll get all the electricity working again, and they'll start growing good food again. It'll take a few years, though. We'll have to go too if we don't get that train.'

'So if Pierce hadn't come,' said Edgar slowly, working it out, 'we wouldn't have got away. We'd have to go too?'

'I guess you're right,' said Chris.

'Are we going to be climrefs?' asked Edgar.

Chris didn't answer. Danny put a hand on Edgar's shoulder.

'Yes,' Danny said. 'We're all climrefs now. Let's go.'

Look out for these other great titles in the *Shades* series:

Animal Lab

by Malcolm Rose

Jamie hates the fact he's gone bald. But can it be right that the animal lab where he works is using monkeys to find a cure?

Mind's Eye

by Gillian Philip

Braindeads like Conor are scary. Or that's what Lara used to think....

Four Degrees More

by Malcolm Rose

When Leyton Curry watches his house fall into the sea, there's nothing he can do.

But then he realises global warming's to blame. And the more he learns, the angrier he gets...

Life of the Party

by Gillian Philip

Chloe's life and soul of the party. After all a little drink never hurt anyone.

But if Chloe's having this much fun, why does it feel as though she's crying inside?

Man Trap
by Tish Farrell

Danny doesn't want to be a hunter, but the rains have failed and he and his father must go out poaching or his family will starve. Then Danny makes a fatal mistake...

Danger Money
by Mary Chapman

Bob Thompson is thrilled when he goes to work on the Admiral, an armed smack defending itself against German U boats. But it's not long before he really has to earn his danger money...